Dear Parents:

Congratulations! Your child is taking the first steps on an exciting journey. The destination? Independent reading!

STEP INTO READING® will help your child get there. The program offers five steps to reading success. Each step includes fun stories and colorful art or photographs. In addition to original fiction and books with favorite characters, there are Step into Reading Non-Fiction Readers, Phonics Readers and Boxed Sets, Sticker Readers, and Comic Readers—a complete literacy program with something to interest every child.

Learning to Read, Step by Step!

Ready to Read **Preschool–Kindergarten**
• big type and easy words • rhyme and rhythm • picture clues
For children who know the alphabet and are eager to begin reading.

Reading with Help **Preschool–Grade 1**
• basic vocabulary • short sentences • simple stories
For children who recognize familiar words and sound out new words with help.

Reading on Your Own **Grades 1–3**
• engaging characters • easy-to-follow plots • popular topics
For children who are ready to read on their own.

Reading Paragraphs **Grades 2–3**
• challenging vocabulary • short paragraphs • exciting stories
For newly independent readers who read simple sentences with confidence.

Ready for Chapters **Grades 2–4**
• chapters • longer paragraphs • full-color art
For children who want to take the plunge into chapter books but still like colorful pictures.

STEP INTO READING® is designed to give every child a successful reading experience. The grade levels are only guides; children will progress through the steps at their own speed, developing confidence in their reading. The F&P Text Level on the back cover serves as another tool to help you choose the right book for your child.

Remember, a lifetime love of reading starts with a single step!

To Greg and Connie,
super grandparents!
—C.R.

For all the awesome
grandparents out there
—A.E.

Text copyright © 2022 by Candice Ransom
Cover art and interior illustrations copyright © 2022 by Ashley Evans

Visit us on the Web!
StepIntoReading.com
rhcbooks.com

Educators and librarians, for a variety of teaching tools, visit us at RHTeachersLibrarians.com

Library of Congress Cataloging-in-Publication Data is available upon request.
ISBN 978-0-593-30263-7 (trade) — ISBN 978-0-593-30264-4 (lib. bdg.) — ISBN 978-0-593-30265-1 (ebook)

Printed in the United States of America
10 9 8 7 6 5 4 3 2 1
First Edition

This book has been officially leveled by using the F&P Text Level Gradient™ Leveling System.

Grandparents Day!

by Candice Ransom
illustrated by Ashley Evans

Random House 🏠 New York

Grandma, Grandpa!
Here they are!

Special day—

hop in their car!

First stop,
breakfast.
Pancake place.

Look! My pancake
has a face.

Next, we go see
dinosaurs.

Above our heads
an airplane soars.

City park has
paddle boats.

Lost my flip-flop!

Hey, it floats!

Last stop is the

hardware store.

SALE

SALE!

Wood,

paint brush,

nails, and more.

Grandparents' house.
Time for lunch!

Fred gets dog treats.

Crunch, crunch, crunch.

Grandpa's workshop.

Building fun.

Paint it purple.

Birdhouse done!

Throw green ball.

Go, Fred, go!

Yucky ball drops
on my toe.

Chicken, green beans, salad, bread.

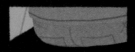

Yummy supper.

Sorry, Fred!

Grandma's brownies,
warm and sweet.

One in each hand.

Which to eat?

Wall becomes a movie screen.

Is that our dad?

Skinny teen!

Animal shapes

we can make.

Rabbit, kitten,
wiggly snake!

Drive home under
stars and moon.

Hugs and kisses.

See you soon!